ruler (can be used as splint if necessary) ↗

This guide is dedicated
to Asa,
an expert on school already!

↑
pencil box
(or emergency
writing rations)

↑
notebook
(or crisis
management
papers)

↑
compass
(not the kind that
helps out in the
wilderness, but useful
for untamed math
problems)

↗
(or critical adhesive
glue stick
support)

Protractor
(for covering all the
angles)
→

Pleasant Company Publications
8400 Fairway Place
Middleton, Wisconsin 53562

Book Design by Amelia

↑
scissors
(to cut to the
chase)

First Pleasant Company Publications Printing,
2002
An Amelia® Book
Manufactured in Singapore
American Girl® is a trademark of Pleasant Company

02 03 04 05 06 07 TWP 10 9 8 7 6 5 4 3 2 1

↑
This is NOT your locker combination — don't forget
to memorize your own or you'll be in trouble!

School is about to start and NO WAY do I want to make the same mistakes that I made last year. So I'm writing this guide to be sure I do things RIGHT.

I'll start with **10** school year resolutions.

1. This year I will NOT call my teacher "Mom" by mistake.

Mom, uh... I mean, Ms. Busby?

cheeks bright red →

stomach suddenly queasy →

floor I want to sink into
↓

I write better, sharper ideas with a nice pencil tip. Blunt tips make my ideas clunky.

2. I solemnly swear that I will always have at least <u>two</u> sharpened pencils with me.

3. I hereby vow to try to get to school early so that I can see my friends before class starts.

Carly

Leah

It will put me in a good mood if I can begin my day talking with Carly and Leah.

4. I promise, cross my heart, to return all my library books on time, so I'll always get to check out new ones.

moldy dark corner

What's <u>this</u> book doing here? I checked it out <u>years</u> ago. I don't want to know what the overdue fine is!

BOO!

ghost book that will haunt you if you don't let its pages rest in peace - in the library!

5. I resolve to invent my own games if I don't have anyone to play with at recess.

6. I vow to care only about <u>my</u> grades, not about what other kids get.

7. I will absolutely try to sit in the front of the class.

8. I pledge to eat a good breakfast EVERY day.

↑ Lumpy oatmeal is NOT a good breakfast.

I swear it's not *me* — it's my stomach.

GEEOOORK! RRRBBOOOGLE!

9. I will try to learn one new vocabulary word a week — <u>and</u> use it!

↑ Stewed prunes are NOT a good breakfast.

Teacher, what's the hermeneutics of book reports?

Is it like the therapeutics of hook sports?

Or the aeronautics of crook forts?

10. I solemnly proclaim that no matter what happens in school this year, I WILL BE PREPARED!

↑ Cold pizza <u>is</u> a good breakfast— yum!

↑ Fresh donut is a VERY good breakfast.

backpack with school supplies, first-aid kit, lunch box, extra clothes, telescope →

also magnifying glass, umbrella, earplugs, nose plugs, and notebook

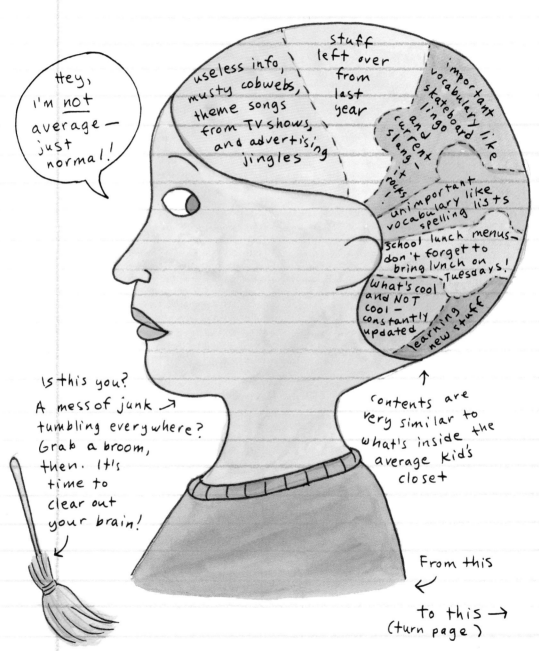

INSIDE THE AVERAGE STUDENT'S BRAIN

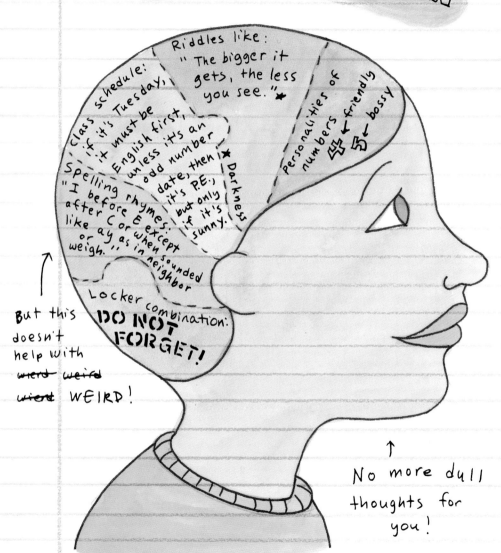

SCHOOL TOOLS

Most schools send home a list of stuff to get for the first day of school, but they don't tell you what you <u>really</u> need:

laser sanitizer for gross school bathrooms

also useful for removing toilet paper stuck to your shoe →

I'll just hold it till I get home.

personal alarm since each clock in the school has a different time on it →

beep! beep!

Is it almost 3:00 or just after 10:00? Morning or afternoon? Hmmmm?

← inflatable gorilla to ward off bullies

Meet my buddy, Kong.

or inflatable alien →

Take me to your leader.

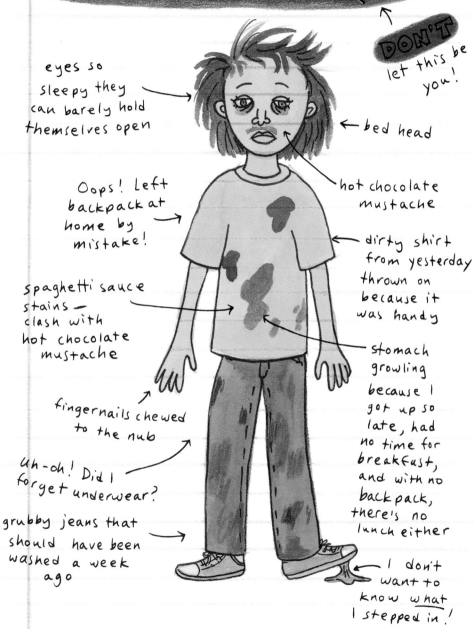

NOT ABC'S

OR HOW TO HANDLE EMERGENCIES...

Band-Aid for paper cuts

To resuscitate your brain after lethal lectures have bored it to death, take DEEP breaths and think of knock-knock jokes. Slowly but surely, your brain will revive.

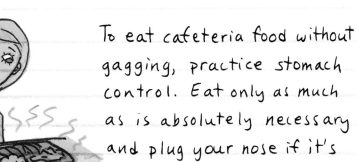

I can't stop yawning!

hot water bottle for cramped hands tired of taking notes

To eat cafeteria food without gagging, practice stomach control. Eat only as much as is absolutely necessary and plug your nose if it's REALLY bad. (Don't look, either.)

Both these cures will work at home, too — use in case of bad home cooking or predictable parental lecture.

BUT S.O.S!

...NOT INVOLVING LOSS OF BLOOD

If someone steals your lunch and you know who the thief is, say something to make them really regret that they ate it.

crutches for foot injured by falling backpack →

→ ice pack for head-ache caused by massive homework

Oh, I hope you didn't eat my lunch by mistake. I have a heart condition, and my mom hides my medicine in my dessert. It doesn't make the food taste bad.

But it <u>could</u> give you a heart attack.

Suddenly, I feel VERY sick!

If someone is mean to you and calls you names, think of the strangest word you can and call them that.

It can be impossible to avoid bullies, but it's NOT impossible to stand up for yourself! ↓

You're a klorgag-fiserket!

↑ no swear-words so you don't get in trouble

Huh?

↑ They'll spend days trying to figure out what it is you called them.

My gorilla's bigger than yours!

eyes barely even blink →

mouth never opens wider than this

gray clothes to match gray voice →

hands ← never gesture- that would be too expressive

← drab shoes with no personality to go with drab everything else

The Monotone Mumbler

This teacher can be recognized chiefly by his <u>voice</u>. He says everything in exactly the same tone, as if he were reading the phone book.

DANGER: You might fall asleep in class! To keep your eyes open, draw a chart of how you wish his voice would rise and fall.

Helpful Hint: wear tight underwear — the pain will keep you awake!

THE rain in Spain falls mainly ON the plain.

to Teachers

The Homework Heaper

This teacher piles on so much homework, you don't have time for ANYTHING else. ~~DON'T~~ groan that it's too much or she might give you more. ("I'll show you too much!") **DO** try bargaining with her.

... and read 35 pages in your science book. Don't forget the 6-page essay due tomorrow.

never met a handout she didn't like – and use!

sensible, no-nonsense shoes →

exhausted eyes with deep bags

Can I trade two pages of homework today for four pages on Friday?

Is it possible that we can do more work in class and less at home?

Helpful Hint: Try sleeping in this class — then you'll be fresh for your homework later.

The Gruff Grump

Make my day! Just give me any excuse to give you a detention.

This teacher has been working too hard for too long. Don't get on his bad side. (I know, you're asking what other side is there?) And try not to be grumpy yourself or things will get even worse.

mouth always scowling

red pen always ready in his pocket

Helpful Hint: Try whatever you can to cheer him up. He might lose some of his gruffness. (But I don't promise it.)

maybe shoes are too tight and pointy, and that's why he's so grouchy

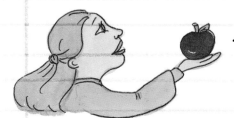

I thought you might like an apple.

Is it poisoned?

The Doormat Teacher

This teacher is usually (but not always) a substitute. You can tell a Doormat by her inability to control kids. Having students run the class can be fun for a day or two, but gets BOOOOOOORING after a while.

DANGER: Doormats can go from being walked all over to being run all over — watch out for stampedes!

Helpful Hint: Protect this delicate endangered species by telling the other students to listen to her — show her your respect.

The Perfect Teacher

This is not a mythological creature, but a rare breed indeed. You'll be lucky to have 1 specimen from this genus in all the years you go to school. But one is all you need, because this teacher is so exciting you'll never forget her. You'll recognize her by her ability to open up your brain to completely new things.

head full of terrific ideas

usually holding something interesting

even more likely to have a book in her hand — books are one of her favorite things

It's hard not to love this teacher — so go ahead!

Helpful Hint: You may not recognize this species at first — they can be camouflaged, but with time their talents shine!

She'll have you doing stuff you never thought you could do — and that's a great lesson in itself!

INTERPRETING

Talking to teachers can be like talking to another species!

"This won't count for a grade." = Oh, yes it does!

"This will take a little extra work." = Better spend the whole weekend on it!

"Extra credit" = You get a second chance — don't blow it!

"Standardized test" = long, boring test where the first question is "Do you have the right kind of pencil to take the test in the first place?"

"Work independently at home." = If your project doesn't have lumps of glue and sloppy corners, I'll know a grown-up did it.

TEACHER TALK

"I'm disappointed with how you did this." = You have to do it over.

↑
Do you plant stink bombs in class?

"Is that clear? Any questions?" = Ask now or forever hold your peace.

"Class, I have a special surprise today!" = Today we're seeing a filmstrip on mushroom spores.

Do you pass notes often?

"I want to see your work on these math problems." = No chicken-scratches allowed. You'd better make those numbers look like numbers!

Wasn't the War of 1812 in 1812?

"Teachers don't have favorites." = If I have a favorite, I'm definitely not telling you!

↑
Do you point out your teacher's mistakes?

If you answered yes to any of these, chances are good that you're NOT a teacher's pet! →

PURRRR

What Kind of

1. What kind of mood do you need to be in to do homework?

Do you cover your books with: ↓

↑ wallpaper?

A. calm and collected	B. happy, listening to music	C. utter desperation
"Books here, paper there, pens over there – all set!"	"I write better to the beat."	"AWK! This is all due TOMORROW!"

2. What do you do when the teacher asks for someone to go first for an oral report?

↑ paper bags?

A. Raise your hand so you can get it over with.	B. Look at the person next to you as a likely candidate.	C. Suddenly need to go to the bathroom.
"Might as well..."	"You go, you go, you go..."	"It's definitely time to go!"

← fly paper?

3. What do you do when you forget your homework?

A. Admit that you forgot it	B. Give an inventive excuse	C. Tell your mom you're too sick to go to school
"I'm sorry!"	"I was abducted by aliens and only returned in time to make it to school!"	"I have a horrible headache and I'm seeing spots!"

Is your back-pack:

↓

↑

light and easy to carry? (you've got to be dreaming! What school do you go to?)

4. What do you do when you know the answer to a question?

A. Raise your hand and wait to be called on	B. Lean forward and wave your hand wildly	C. Blurt out the answer, you're so excited to know it
eager-eyed and polite ↙	"Oh, oh, oh! I know! I know! Pick me!"	"It's Godzilla!"

↑ heavier than you?

"It's a tough job, but someone's got to do it."

on rollers and pulled by a weight-lifter, it's so hard to budge

5. For extra credit, you always choose projects that are...

6. If you're running late for school, you skip...

your favorite non-school supply is: →

dried noodles for art projects

felt – you can use it a zillion ways

dry ice – cool for creepy effects!

7. How do you treat substitute teachers?

A. You help them with the class routine.	B. You help them with the class routine.	C. You help them with the class routine.
We usually have 15 minutes of silent reading now.	We're doing special research on recess now, so we're supposed to have an extra hour outside.	I have a private tutoring session now — I'll see you tomorrow! Bye!

If you answered mostly A's:

   You're a perfect student. Teachers love you. You may even be a teacher's pet.

If you answered mostly B's:

   If your teacher has a sense of humor, you get along fine. If your teacher is a grump — watch out! And if your mom sits in on your class one day, you're in trouble!

If you answered mostly C's:

   Sorry, you're <u>not</u> the teacher's pet. Try participating more. You might have more fun if you were more "there" there.

NOTES ON

DON'T

take notes on messy scraps of paper you're just going to lose.

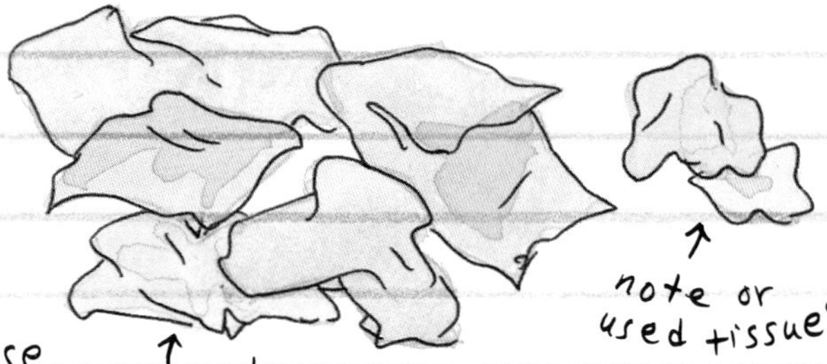

Fold up as tiny as possible.

DON'T

write so sloppily you can't read what you've written.

Don't throw paper, but drop it UNOBTRUSIVELY near your friend.

DON'T

copy someone else's notes. You'll just make their mistakes instead of your own.

Oops! I don't mean THESE kinds of notes!

NOTE - TAKING

DO keep your notes in the same predictable place, so you'll always know where to find them.

I always keep my notes in the refrigerator — they stay fresh and crisp that way.

DO write notes that are useful.

Let's see — should I write down what the teacher is wearing?

How about the weather? It's such a nice day today.

Or jokes? I like those...

DO bother to read your notes again before the test — otherwise why take them?

These are so good, they're worth reading year after year

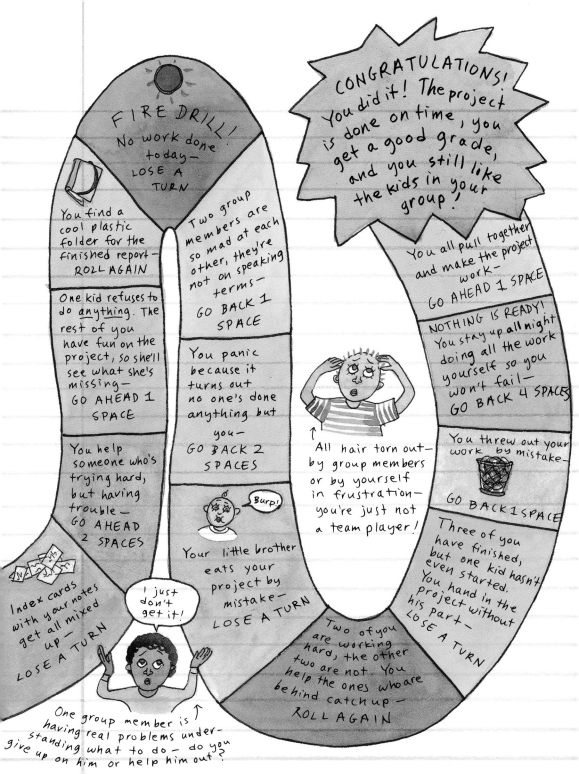

Nimble

Numbers can be tricky to deal with — they're wily and elusive. But here are some hints to help you tame these capricious beasts. You can't treat all numbers alike (or you do so at your own peril). It's essential to understand each number's nature, so you can handle it right.

Grrr!

Fives may look jolly — until they bare their teeth! Don't be fooled! They're often snappish and bite, especially when by themselves. In groups, they're easier to approach.

I wuv you!

Twos look a lot like fives upside-down and backwards, but they're completely different in temperament. Known for their sweet, cuddly nature, twos make wonderful pets.

Fours are the fairest of numbers. They make terrific judges and can intervene if there's a fight between other numbers.

Well, it can be this way...

...or I see how it can be that way.

Think of all the things there are seven of — seven seas...

seven days of the week, seven wonders of the world...

Sevens love to have fun. They think they're lucky — and they're right! The more sevens you have, the better!

Numbers

Eights are the joke-tellers of the number family. It's always great to have an → eight around!

Did you hear why six is afraid of seven?

Because seven eight nine!

And what did the zero say to the eight?

"Nice belt you've got!"

Aren't you ecstatic to have me around?

Ones are complete snobs. They think they're first in everything. Flattery goes a long way with them. Otherwise, watch out! Their vanity is easily offended.

YAWN! Is it a school day today?

Nines are a bit slow, as if they're → always half-asleep. But with some prodding, you can get them to work for you.

pleeeze don't hurt me! pleeeze.

Sixes are worrywarts and fearful of everything. Don't make sudden moves or they'll faint in terror. If you're gentle, you can keep a six calm and under control. If you're not, it can be a disaster!

Let's go bungee jumping! Wheeee!

Threes are unpredictable. Sometimes they behave well. Other times they're absolutely wild. You can <u>never</u> control them, but you won't be bored with them, either.

What kind of test-

Take __this__ test (it's easy!) to find the answer.

1. Before a test, you...

Do you line up a row of freshly sharpened pencils?
↓

2. When you start a test, you...

Or do you prefer high-tech tools?
↓

← combination mechanical pencil, stopwatch, ink-eraser, and toothbrush

After a test do you look like this? →

"What hit me?"

This? →

"Just finish me off now!"

"Phew! That's done!"

Or this? ↑

5. When you finish a test, you. . .

A. chant a charm to ensure success.	B. feel sick because you've chewed your pencil down to the stub.	C. check your answers to make sure you haven't missed anything.

"Wugga wugga boo boo, wugga wugga boo boo, wugga wugga boo bo..."

"Bleh!"

"Looking good!"

6. When you get your test back, you. . .

A. give out bubble gum cigars, you're so proud and happy.	B. wait until you can't stand it anymore, then look at your grade.	C. look calm on the outside, but on the inside, you're cheering.

"Have one to celebrate! It's a big, bouncy, healthy "A"!"

"Do I dare?"

"Hmmm, nice..."

"YAY!!"

← gold star for good work

happy face for a job well done

If you answered mostly A's:
you rely on luck too much — start using your brain! This is school, not a lottery!

If you answered mostly B's:
you're not relying on _anything_ — no wonder you're so worried. Start studying and you'll feel a LOT better!

If you answered mostly C's:
you're a test-taking expert — congratulations! (And can you help me study for my next test, please?)

What I'd like to see on tests ↘

ALIEN GOOD JOB FOR AN EARTHLING CREDIT EXTRA

COUPON

GOOD FOR 1 SLICE OF PIZZA

↑ seal of approval

HISTORY

DON'T make a hash out of names and dates. History can be your friend! Add these handy-dandy ingredients to any history report and you'll earn extra points — money back guaranteed!*

For extra spice and sizzle include at least one famous name and what that person might have said about whatever it is you're writing.

for example
↓

"As Columbus would have seen it, there was no point in building the Great Wall of China." Why cross on land when you can go by boat?"

or
↓

George Washington felt lucky he wasn't in London during the Great Plague. "Ooh, yuck, gross — I hate nasty diseases like that! Wooden teeth are bad enough."

* That is, I guarantee you'll want your money back, but too bad, it'll be too late for that! Now isn't that a lesson worth learning in itself?

HELPER

To add meat to your report, don't forget to put in details about daily life. Kings and queens are important, but so are peasants and servants.

I didn't say "Let them eat cake." I said this wig is killing me!

And with all the tea dumped into Boston Harbor, what were we supposed to drink?

servant girl

↑ Marie Antoinette

That's when I invented lemonade— yum!

The secret ingredient for your report can be a drawing, a map, a chart— make it something fun!

postage stamp from Pony Express (Hey! Were bicycles invented back then?)

actual replica of ticket for the Titanic

Admit One (No Icebergs Allowed.)

ORAL REPORTS

To face this beast, you need a cool head, calmness in the face of adversity, and great courage.

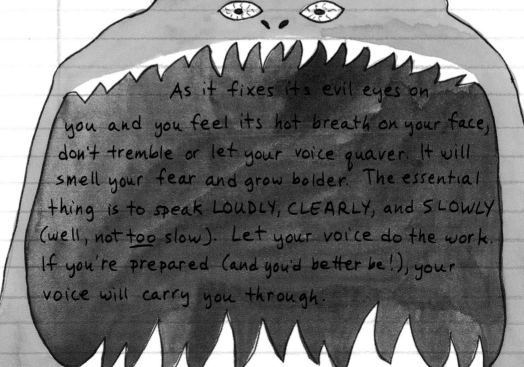

As it fixes its evil eyes on you and you feel its hot breath on your face, don't tremble or let your voice quaver. It will smell your fear and grow bolder. The essential thing is to speak LOUDLY, CLEARLY, and SLOWLY (well, not _too_ slow). Let your voice do the work. If you're prepared (and you'd better be!), your voice will carry you through.

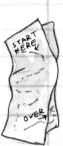

STEP ONE: Use a compass! Follow a map! It's imperative (that means VERY important) that you know where you're going (with your words, that is). Don't ramble, don't say "um, um, um," don't stray from the direct path. One false step a n d

Also, get inoculated against sleeping sickness, dropsies, and stomach terrors.

EEEEEEEEEEEE

YOU'LL FALL INTO THE GAPING MOUTH OF THE BEAST!

Unless you're very confident and experienced, write your whole talk out and practice it. Notes are not enough. But read your report like you're talking to a friend. Otherwise, it'll be BOOORING. And bored beasts can be NASTY!

STEP TWO: Know your stuff! Know what you're talking about, and you can actually relax and have fun. The monster may still be threatening, its teeth may still be sharp, but facing your fears can be

EXHILARATING!

Especially when you feel up to the task, trained, and ready to go!

Wheee! It's a snap!

Wow! Oral reports are more fun than bungee jumping!

You're not terrified of me?

SPICE UP

YOUR BOOK REPORT

← Bare-bones book report is like a stick figure.

Adding details gives more personality. →

Recipe for sweet success:

1. Add details! Don't just say you like a character, say you like his twinkly eyes or her hopscotch skills — give a reason why.

2. Explain how the book made you feel (bored, sad, happy, nervous, hungry — maybe it's a cookbook) and what parts made you feel that way most.

3. Is there something in the book you would change? The ending? A character? The useful information at the back of the book?

4. Pretend you're reviewing the book for other kids. Who do you think should read it? Why?

sour
lemon
↓

↑
sour
grapes

↑
sweet
and
sour

Read it because I SAID SO!

↑
This approach won't work.

Then he heard a knock. Then he opened the door. Then he saw it. Then he screamed. Then it ate him.

...then I fell asleep.

Recipe for extra-spicy reports:
1. Don't say "then" and "then" and "then" unless you want to put your reader to sleep. Try writing your report as if it were an argument between two people or as if it were a news story on something that really happened.

Reporting live from Alabama, where a blind-deaf girl has shown the world she can break down the walls between herself and others.

She's Helen Keller!

2. Try making a comic strip book report for something really different.

Yessir, I'm having sooo much fun painting!

Wow, Tom, can I try, please?

Well, I dunno.

Maybe

Please, let me try! Just a little! Please, please, please, please, PLEASE.

Oh, go ahead!

Add as many sound effects as you can.

GLOBAL

BASIC MAP READING

↑ up means north

↓ down means south

← left means west

→ right means east

↑ Use a compass if you're still having problems.

Map folding is a whole 'nother skill. ↓

↑ Lay out map.

O.K., good enough — you can now read any map with ease and clarity. Memorizing countries, states, and their capitals is something else entirely.

↑ Fold along lines.

↑ Give up and crumple whole thing into ball.

How to make a model of the world: ↓

↑ the flat model— use a giant lollipop (No licking until after you're graded!)

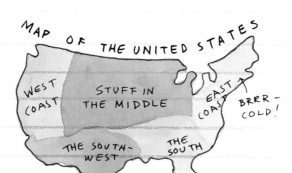

MAP OF THE UNITED STATES

WEST COAST

STUFF IN THE MIDDLE

EAST COAST ↑

BRRR— COLD!

THE SOUTH-WEST

THE SOUTH

↑ PHEW— HOT!

← the round model— markers on a balloon work great — but keep away from porcupines

Can I have that pretty balloon?

NO!

UNDERSTANDING

World Factoids
↓

Howdy!

↑
Penguins live in Antarctica, not the Arctic.

↑
A roll is a continental breakfast.

Wish you were here!

↑
Polar bears live in the Arctic, not Antarctica.

BASIC GEOGRAPHY

A continent is a big land mass (but a continental breakfast is a very small breakfast).

<u>A</u> country can be big or little. <u>The</u> country is where there are farms.

MOoo!

I'm from the country, but I live <u>in</u> the country of Switzerland.

There, that's as basic as you can get. If you want to know where Surinam is or which country is the biggest, better get yourself an atlas, not a survival guide.

Two-hump camels come from Asia. →

I'm better!

No, <u>I</u> am!

More World Factoids
↓

Earth is 3/4 water— way more ocean than land! ↓

That's good news if you're a fish!

But there are more insects than any other creatures. ↓

So there, fishies!

One-hump camels come from Africa. ←

Creativity Crunch

Don't take a bite — it's not that kind of crunch!

No, I'm not talking about a candy bar, but about that tight feeling your head gets when your teacher expects you to be creative ON DEMAND. Teachers think assignments like "write a poem or a story" are easy. Ha! It's not like you just switch on a button and become instantly full of great ideas.

← the eater

I'll think of something AFTER this snack.

the sensitive soul

You can't command genius — you simply wait for it to strike.

the organizer

I must wait for the muse to visit me.

I'll do my math homework first. At least that has a clear beginning and end.

SENSATIONAL

No volcanoes or plants allowed!

Why settle for the ordinary when you can have the EXTRAordinary? Here are some science fair projects I'd like to see!

MAKE A ROBOT

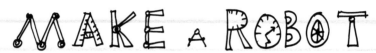

Think these projects aren't realistic? How about just doing *part* of them?

Then train it to do all your homework AND clean your room!

SHOVING CLOTHES UNDER THE BED IS NOT PROPER CLEANING. I WILL SHOW YOU HOW IT SHOULD BE DONE.

Feel the muscle here!

↑ not a whole robot, but a robotic arm

TRAIN YOUR HAMSTER

With careful scientific methods, teach your pet to perform amazing tricks and demonstrate a profound understanding of human speech.

START

So what you're saying is that you want me to run through the maze and find the peanut? All that work for just a goober? Are you nuts?

↑ or simpler yet, a circuit— connect the wires and light the bulb!

Science

Invent a flying machine.

Look! I'm a giant bat — I'm Batkid!

Or simply test which kite shapes fly better.

traditional kite

Discover a new species of dinosaur. (Well, why not?)

looks → suspiciously like an old traffic cone

Here's my re-creation of Dinodon, the dinosaur whose giant tooth I excavated in a parking lot.

box kite

fancy sun kite

Build your own dinosaur out of junk.

the newly discovered prehistoric trashadon

Which paper airplane goes farther?

TO BRING LUNCH

← paper   or plastic →

   If you pack a lunch, these guidelines will ensure a safe, pleasant eating experience. You're already a step ahead, since at least you know you won't get food poisoning from the cafeteria.

   Look at the bench BEFORE you sit down.

Hey! That's my donut!

   Don't sit next to anyone who sticks straws up his nose.

Wait, wait! I can get buffalo wings up my nose, too! Wanna see?

Don't trade food unless you know what you're getting.

Hey, are those tentacles?

I thought you said tuna fish, not jellyfish — or octopus!

OR NOT TO  BRING LUNCH

edible or inedible?

If you're a real daredevil and willing to risk your stomach with cafeteria food, you'd better observe the following rules:

Oops!

Keep an extra shirt in your backpack so if the sloppy joe is _really_ sloppy, you don't have to wear sauce all day.

← Extra pants and shoes could be handy, too.

No matter how hungry you are, don't eat anything you can't identify.

Mold is NOT a good sign. Suspicious lumps are to be avoided and if it's moving, don't put it on your fork!

HOW TO AVOID THE

Do I look fat?

If the pictures are taken after lunch, make sure there's **NOTHING** between your teeth.

o o o

Lunch was yummy today!

DON'T get your hair cut the day before Picture Day.

o o o

It'll grow out— I HOPE!

o o o

Is this ME?

DON'T let your friend give you a makeover — you might end up looking like an alien.

School Photo

CHEESE!

CHEESIER!

DON'T wear itchy clothes, no matter how cool they look.

If I can just reach that spot - quick before he snaps the photo.

When the photographer says, "Say cheese," **DON'T** think of stinky, grown-up type cheese or you'll look like you ← smell something nasty!

How can anyone eat cheese that smells like dirty socks?

DON'T look so fake no one can tell it's you.

Now I look better than me!

FIELD TRIP

Stop when red lights flash! →

Places I'd love to go to, but we NEVER do: ↓

candy factory ↓

↑

I've always wondered if jelly beans REALLY have jelly or beans in them.

teddy bear hospital ↳

Avoid getting assigned a partner who gets carsick easily.

I'm sorry, but I can't be Cleo's partner. I'm allergic to her shampoo. Really!

Don't pack extra stuff in your backpack that you'll never use.

Huff, puff! Why did I think I'd need a blow-dryer, a flashlight, and a snakebite kit in the art museum?

A deck of cards, however, is always handy.

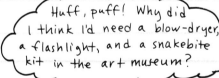

Wow! We're there already!

← Lonely, sick teddies deserve hugs, too!

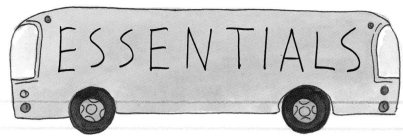

ESSENTIALS

Don't ask embarrassing questions.

Why would anyone CHOOSE to study mushrooms? Sounds boring to me.

How much do you get paid?

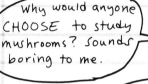

fortune cookie factory ↓

How DO they get the fortunes inside — and WHO writes them, anyway?

Don't touch ANYTHING unless you're invited to.

Oopsy-daisy!

RARE VASE

CRASH!

mad scientist's laboratory →

why aren't kids ever invited to places like that? →

Don't volunteer unless you know what you're getting into.

See what happens when 250 volts of static electricity shoots through Leo's body!

1. The best conditions for you to do homework are:

You like your home- work to be:

portable ↓

↑
easy-carry case — no big, heavy textbook

| A. at a neat, organized desk. | B. while eating a snack and watching TV. | C. while on safari in Africa. |

"Now I can concentrate."

"I need to do at least 2 other things along with home-work."

"Ah, the great outdoors!"

2. You like to do homework...

| A. as soon as you get home from school. | B. after you've had a chance to relax for a while. | C. right before it's due. |

"I'm home, so I'd better get to it."

"I'll start that report after this show."

"If only the bus ride was a little longer..."

edible ↓

← Spanish mission made of brownies— yum!

3. In your work, you try to do...

| A. the best you possibly can. | B. as little as possible. | C. the fun parts. |

You like projects that:

involve clay

4. The time you didn't finish your homework, it was because...

map of somewhere (not sure exactly where)

| A. you were sick. | B. you forgot. | C. you **never** finish your homework. |

have more than one use

It's a volcano for a science project, but also a model of Vesuvius for history, **and** an original sculpture for art!

which of the following counts as homework?

 ← cleaning toilets

folding laundry →

 ↑ gluing macaroni on cardboard

5. Your favorite kind of homework is...

A. long reports that you can put in a fancy folder.

Now that looks professional!

B. projects.

Ta-da! The Alamo made of Jell-O!

C. personal research in uncharted territory.

At last I can discover how many licks it takes to finish a giant lollipop!

If you answered mostly A's:
   Homework is no problem for you — you're an expert and can juggle 3 projects at a time.

If you answered mostly B's:
   You're creative in doing your homework — especially in thinking of ways NOT to do it!

If you answered mostly C's:
   Homework and you are not always compatible, but you have a great sense of adventure.

FAMOUS PROJECTS

IN THE ANNALS OF HOMEWORK HISTORY

↰ Lindsay's diorama of her backyard for her wilderness project

Clive's dust bunny exhibit↱ for the science fair

↰ Stella's model of the Empire State Building made out of Life Savers (sucked-on, of course)

Ben's banana-peel-and-toothpick architectural design ↑

The back of every notebook has stuff that's supposed to be handy for school. Well, I finally here's a REAL page of: →

USEFUL INFO

Table of Food Measure

All you need to know is which day is Pizza Day — ignore all other cafeteria offerings (or you'll be sorry!)

DON'T try the shepherd's pie — it might have a shepherd in it! →

Table of Homework

(or Homework Table unless you do your homework on the floor)

← one worksheet = ½ hour

← one book report = stalling for an hour, then working for an hour

$4a + 2a =$
$6a - 3a =$
$1.3 \times 2.5 =$
$6.8 \times 7.1 =$

← twenty math problems = misery all afternoon and time calculating that could have been spent watching TV

Table of Linear Measure

The line you're in is always the longest and the slowest.

Worst lines: lining up for the bus, for field trips, for lunch

Best lines: lining up for fire drills

Ball Chart

← The less round the ball, the less it will bounce.

↑
DON'T pick a ball that looks like a whoopy cushion!

BBRRRNG! BBRRNG!

WAKE UP! TIME FOR SCHOOL!

Table of Time Measure

Monday — Ugh! Have to get up early again.

Tuesday — Groan! A whole week of school ahead.

Wednesday — Stuck right in the middle of the week.

Thursday — Hey, this is getting to be fun!

Friday — Yay! A great day AND the weekend ahead!

Saturday — PERFECT! A day all for me!

Sunday — Can't enjoy it knowing that tomorrow is ... MONDAY again!

I've graduated from:

← Mr. Google-eyes

lunchboxes with characters on them

← to insulated high-tech containers in fashion colors

I've gone from thick markers, drawing like this →

I used to → have easy, fun homework

connect-the-dots ↗

So! Now you're all set for school. You won't be swallowed by oral reports, poisoned by cafeteria food, or trampled by wild science projects. You may have close calls and near misses, but YOU WILL SURVIVE!

to cool gel pens, drawing like this ↓

↑ hands behind back to avoid drawing them

notice relaxed smile, not tense or worried at all! →

now I have tons of hard work ↓

HELP!

↖ prepared survivalist with backpack, hard hat, emergency supply kit, and, most important of all, brain packed with skills and tips to face any school horror

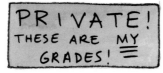

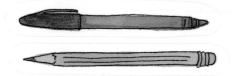

EMERGENCY WRITING RATIONS

STEPS TO TAKE TO SCHOOL CROSSING

BRAINSTORM!

EMERGENCY
Pink
Pearl !
PAPER REPAIR

MUTATED FOOD
EAT AT OWN RISK

ALIEN EXTRA CREDIT
GOOD JOB, EARTHLING!

WASH GYM
CLOTHES NOW!

COUPON
GOOD FOR ONE SLICE PIZZA
GOOD WORK!

TEST TODAY
PANIC BUTTON

LIBRARY BOOKS DUE— GO FIND THEM!

UH, OH - RED PEN - AVOID IT!

TURN ON YOUR BRAIN !

BZZZZZZZ
SPELLING BEE
QUICK - SPELL
WEIRD WIERD WEIRS

GOOD WORK
SEAL OF APPROVAL

RAINBOW STARS FOR STELLAR WORK

TAME THE ORAL REPORT WILD BEAST!

CONGRATULATIONS!

Certificate of Certification

This certifies that

_____

has studied Amelia's useful School Survival Guide and learned to avoid, defeat, or escape all manner of menaces.

GRADE
A

FREE WITH CERTIFICATE
SCHOOL STICKERS

Does homework horrify you? Do oral reports leave you weak in the knees? Do you suffer from the smells of cafeteria food? Then you need <u>Amelia's School Survival Guide</u>. Amelia's advice, games, and quizzes will help you cope with any school worries that come your way. PLUS: 38 Amelia stickers to peel and use!

Here's what Amelia fans have to say:

"Every time I'm in trouble, under pressure, or under-going a lot of stress, your books help me get away from my problems. I end up helping Amelia solve <u>her</u> problems!"
—Angela Fisher

Does that mean you'll do my home-work for me?

"I think your creativity has gone past 1,000 percent. Seriously!"
—Elizabeth Wolfe

I wish I got that percent on my math quiz!

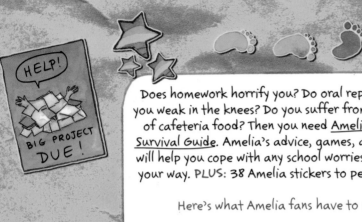

BK047B42BB

Manufactured
in Singapore
ISBN 1-58485-509-6

9 781584 855095

Ages 8 and up
55096 $7.95

7 23232 05509 8

UH, OH — RED PEN — AVOID IT!